POSSUM'S HARVEST MOON

Words and pictures by Anne Hunter

SCHOLASTIC INC.

New York Toronto London Auckland Sydney

ISBN 0-590-76972-3

12 11   8 9/0

Printed in the U.S.A.   08
First Scholastic printing, October 1997

To my Mother and Father

Possum awoke one autumn evening. Shining through the grass was the biggest, brightest, yellowest moon. "Oh!" said Possum, "the harvest moon! What a perfect night for a party. One last dance in the moonlight before the long winter. A Harvest Soiree!" Possum hung the grass with lanterns and berries. Then he hurried off to invite his guests.

"Mice! Mice!" Possum cried at the meadow's edge. "Come to my Harvest Moon Party!"

"We must gather seeds for the winter," said the mice. "We are too busy to come to your party."

Next Possum peered into a pile of leaves. "Come out crickets! Hop along to my party under the bright harvest moon."

"We are tired from singing all summer," said the crickets. "The night air is too cold now and this leaf pile is so snug."

Down by the creek Possum found Raccoon catching fish.
"Dry your hands, Old Raccoon, and come to the last hurrah
of the year."

"Oh, I would, I would," growled Raccoon, "but I
must be good and fat for the long winter. So much to eat,
so little time."

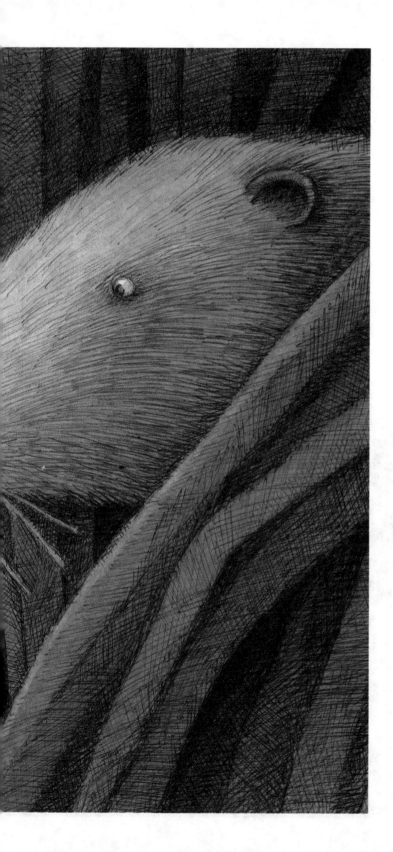

Possum followed the creek to the pond.

"Frogs! Frogs!" Possum shouted. "Come sing and dance under the great, great moon. Come to my Harvest Soiree!"

"Too late, too late, too late!" chorused the frogs. "It's time for us to go underground for the winter."

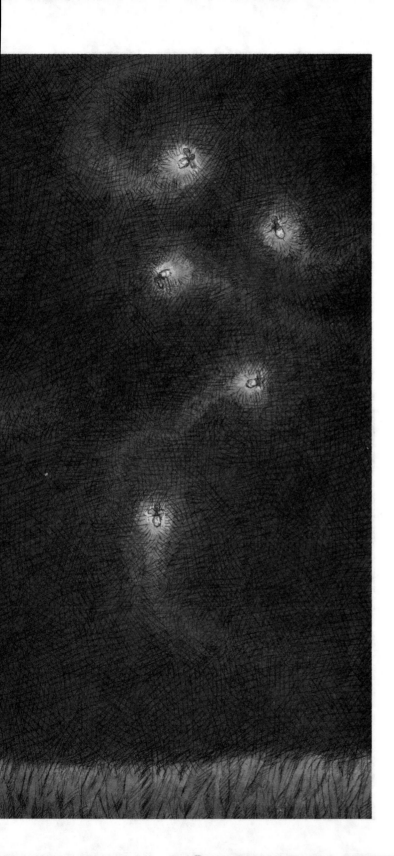

Possum turned sadly toward home.
He looked up to the twinkling sky.
   "Oh, fireflies! Can you . . . could
you come to my party?"
   The fireflies twinkled silently back
at him.

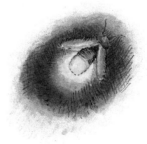

"How could they work on such
a beautiful night?" Possum asked
himself. "How can they think of
sleep in such moonlight?"

He put on his hat and sat alone,
looking up at the great harvest moon.

The great harvest moon rose higher. It shone down
through the grass and under the leaves.
It made every tired and busy creature pause.

It was a moon that made them dream of dancing, of
eating and singing. Toes twitched and voices hummed.
How could they possibly miss Possum's Harvest Soiree?

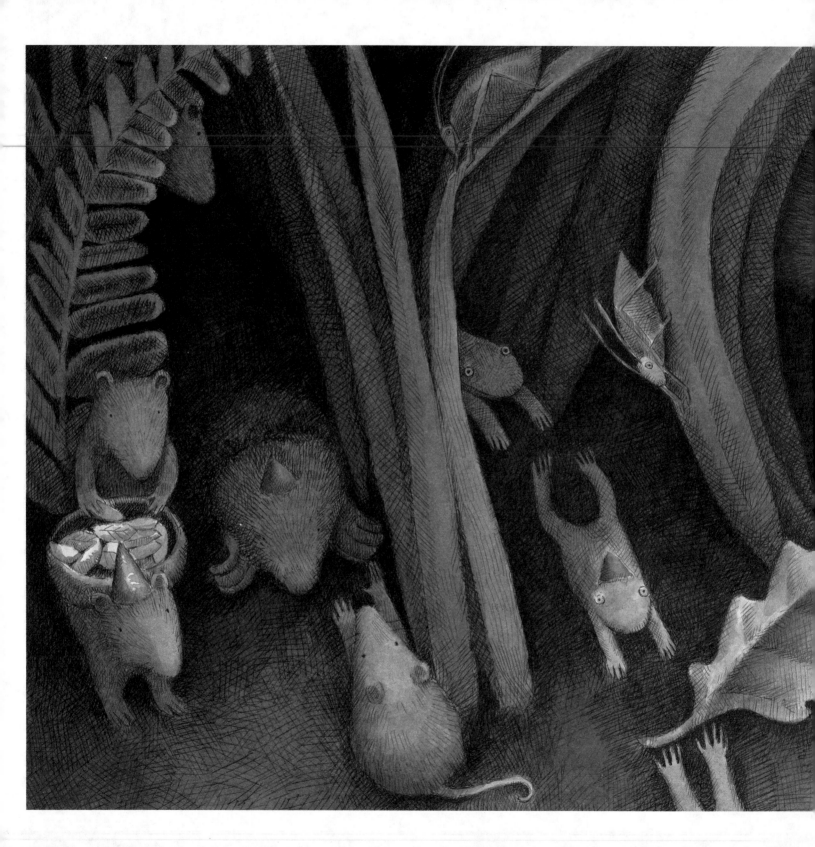

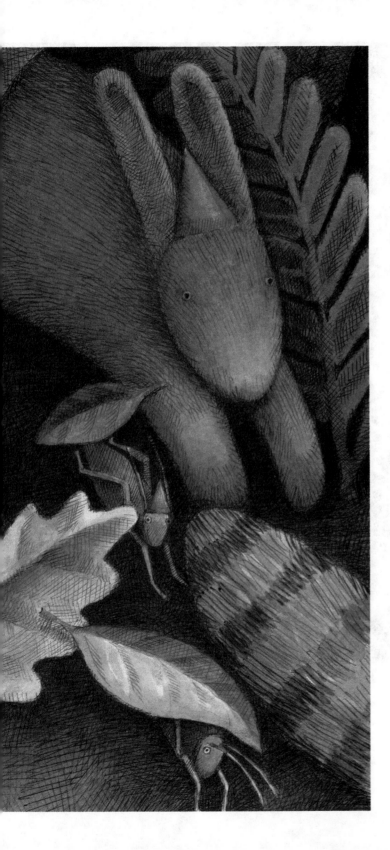

Raccoon rousted his crony, Rabbit. The crickets invited their cousins the katydids. The mice brought the moles. The peepers hopped after the frogs.

They hurried and scurried while the night was still young.

Possum could hear squeaking and scampering from all directions.

And the guests arrived! They brought seeds and berries, fiddles and songs. All together they gazed up at the face of the great harvest moon.

Rabbit and Raccoon settled in down by the food. They nibbled and nodded. "Never, never in all our years," they agreed, "has the harvest moon been so bright. No, never."

The mice danced until the crickets played every jig twice,
and the frogs grew hoarse from singing. The fireflies' lights
flickered and dimmed.

A cool breeze ruffled over the tired creatures as the moon
sank low. It was time to go home. Home to dens and nests,
holes and burrows. Time for winter's long sleep.

"Good night!" squeaked the mice.

"Great party!" chirped the crickets.

"Until next spring," growled
Old Raccoon.

"Farewell!" piped the frogs.

"See you next year!" said Possum.
He waved until every last guest
was gone.

Possum curled up in his own snug home. He looked out to see the
last light of the great moon peeking through the grass.
"Good night," yawned Possum, "good night."